Children's Books:
WHO NEEDS A HUG?

Sally Huss

ISBN 10: 1945742011
ISBN 13: 9781945742019

A koala bear awoke one morning. Feeling magnanimous and grand, he decided to do something generous. So, he called out to anyone who could hear him, "Who needs a hug?"

"Hmmm, a hug?" wondered a passing hippo. "Is it free?"

"Yes indeed and I'll give it with all my heart."

"Why not?" said the hippo coolly.

So the koala scampered down from his eucalyptus tree…

… spread his arms as wide as he could and gave the hippo a hug he would never forget.

"Very nice," said the hippo, and then ambled off.

"Who needs a hug?" called the koala into the forest.

"I could use one," said a giraffe, who poked his head through the trees.

So the koala shimmied up the giraffe's neck, closed his eyes…

… and gave the giraffe a hug he would never forget.

"Thanks so much. Most hugs are kind of skimpy; yours was perfect," said the giraffe, as he lowered his head to let the koala down to the ground. Then he went back to munching leaves on top of the acacia trees.

"Who needs a hug?" the koala called into the forest again.

"I'll have one," said a porcupine sauntering down the lane.

"No one ever hugs me."

"Oh," sighed the kind-hearted koala. "I'll give you a hug you'll never forget. But, keep your quills down."

"I will. I will," promised the porcupine, excited to receive the koala's hug.

The koala snuggled up to the porcupine, gingerly placed his arms around her and squeezed just enough to be felt, but not too much to be pricked.

"That was lovely," she said. "That's a hug I'll never forget."

The koala was happy with the results he was getting. After all, he was putting his whole heart into it.

He wondered who else would like a hug. So he called out,

"Who needs a hug?"

A brown bear answered, "What are you doing?"

"I'm giving away bear hugs," said the koala.

"But you're not a real bear," pointed out the brown bear.

"No one knows that," said the koala. "Besides the hugs are really good."

"Well, okay. I'll try one. Is there any charge?"

"Not at all," said the koala. "But, you'll have to bend down."

The real bear stooped over to let the koala place his arms
around his large neck. The koala closed his eyes, and hugged.

"That's a hug you'll never forget," said the koala.

"I believe you're right," said the brown bear. "Might I have

another?"

"Nope. Just one!"

Then he turned his attention back to the forest and called loudly, "Who needs a hug?"

A forest snake came slithering up. "Any chance I could have one?"

"Of course. Of course," said the kind koala, noting that the snake was not a boa constrictor.

It was a little awkward but the koala managed to wrap his arms around the snake. "This is a hug you'll never forget," promised the koala.

"That's for sure," said the snake, "because a hug is something I never get."

The koala really put his heart into it, realizing that the snake needed a little extra love.

"You're right," said the snake, "I'll never forget it." She wiped a tear from her eye with a shake of her head and wiggled off down the lane.

"Who needs a hug?" the koala called out again.

There was a rustling in the leaves nearby, and who should pop up but a badger. The shy fellow could hardly answer, yet did manage to say, "I do."

"I aim to please," said the koala. "I'm going to give you a hug you'll never forget."

"Oh my," sighed the badger, delighted at the prospect.

Again the koala opened his arms and his heart and tenderly hugged the badger.

"Thank you. Thank you," said the badger. "That will last me my whole life long."

As the koala waved goodbye, his eye caught a tiger lurking in the bushes.

"What's all the fuss about?" asked the tiger.

"I've just been asking if anyone needs a hug," replied the koala.

"Well, I could use a hug," said the tiger.

"Hmmm. I need to think about this," said the koala.

"If you're giving away hugs, I'd like to have one," insisted the tiger. "Besides, I've just eaten. A hug would round off my meal perfectly."

With safety concerns out of the way, the koala placed his arms around the tiger's magnificent head and gave him a hug he would never forget.

"Thank you," said the tiger. Relishing the kindness that he had been shown, he gently set the koala back on the ground.

Saying goodbye to the tiger, the koala was becoming a bit thirsty so he wandered over to a nearby pond.

He drank his fill and then said to whomever might be listening,
"Who needs a hug?"

No one answered. He looked around, then down at the water, saw his reflection and knew the answer. "I do!" he said.

With that, he wrapped his arms around himself and gave himself the biggest hug he had ever given, a hug he would never forget.

This proved to him that you may get a hug from a rabbit, a zebra, or even an impala, but there is no better hug than that from a koala!

Who needs a hug? Everybody needs a hug!

At the end of this book you will find a Certificate of Merit that may be issued to any child who has fulfilled the requirements stated in the Certificate. This fine Certificate will easily fit into a 5"x7" frame, and happily suit any girl or boy who receives it!

Sally writes new books all the time. If you would like to be alerted when one of her new books becomes available or when one of her books is offered FREE, sign up here: http://www.sallyhuss.com/sign-up.html.

Here are a few Sally Huss books you might enjoy. They may be found in soft cover and on Amazon as e-books.

CARE AND FEEDING OF A PET

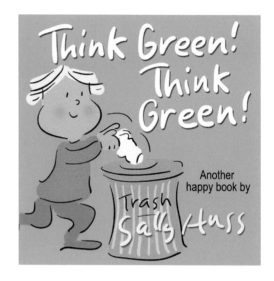

Being Happy and Joyful

Making Good Choices

About the Author/Illustrator

Sally Huss

"Bright and happy," "light and whimsical" have been the catch phrases attached to the writings and art of Sally Huss for over 30 years. Sweet images dance across all of Sally's creations, whether in the form of children's books, paintings, wallpaper, ceramics, baby bibs, purses, clothing, or her King Features syndicated newspaper panel "Happy Musings."

Sally creates children's books to uplift the lives of children and hopes you will join her in this effort by helping spread her happy messages.

Sally is a graduate of USC with a degree in Fine Art and through the years has had 26 of her own licensed art galleries throughout the world.

This certificate may be cut out, framed, and presented to any child who has earned it.

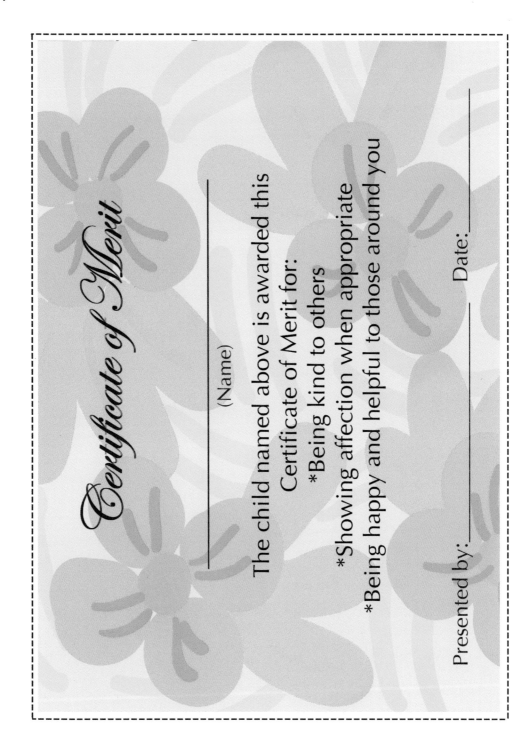

Certificate of Merit

_____
(Name)

The child named above is awarded this Certificate of Merit for:

*Being kind to others

*Showing affection when appropriate

*Being happy and helpful to those around you

Presented by: _____

Date: _____

Printed in Great Britain
by Amazon